Tessa
Our Little Italian Cousin

Mary Hazelton Blanchard Wade

TESSA
Our Little Italian Cousin

CHAPTER I

TESSA

"There comes babbo! There comes babbo!" cried Tessa, as she ran down the narrow street to meet her father, with baby Francesca toddling after her.

The man was not alone,—Beppo and the donkey were with him. They were very tired, for it was a hard trip from the little village on the hilltop to the great city, miles away, and back again. The donkey was not of much help on the homeward journey, either. Poor little patient beast! he was getting old now, and he felt that his day's work was done when he had carried a load of nuts and vegetables to Rome in the morning. But when he had to bring Beppo back again, he felt a little bit sulky. So it was no wonder that he stood quite still every few minutes and did not seem to hear his little master scold.

"Get up, Pietro, get up. We shall be late to supper," Beppo would say, but the donkey would not move till Beppo's father used the whip. He did not strike hard enough to hurt the poor creature, though. Oh no, the kind man would not do that, he was too gentle. But he must make the donkey know the whip was there, or they would never get home.

When they had crossed the wide plain and reached the foot of the hill, Beppo got down and walked. It was too hard on Pietro to make him carry even a little boy now.

They came up the narrow road slowly till they reached the village. And just as the sunset spread over the sky, and gave a glory even to the stones, Tessa caught sight of them.

"My darling Tessa," said her father. "My dear little Francesca." Tired as he was, he took the two children in his arms and hugged them as though he had been away many days. Yet he had left them at five o'clock that very morning.

"We have good news for you, Beppo and I," he went on.

Beppo laughed till the high, pointed hat nearly fell off his head.

"Oh, yes, good news," said Beppo. "You cannot think what it is, Tessa. May I tell her, babbo?"

"Yes, my child," his father answered.

"You are to go to Rome to-morrow with babbo and me. The great artist who buys our fruit wants to see you. He thinks he may want you for a model. And me, too, Tessa, he wants me! He will put us both in a picture. Babbo said you also had long hair, and that we look much alike.

"Only think, Tessa! he will pay babbo for letting him paint us. And mother shall have a new dress, and you shall have some red ribbons. We will all have a feast. Say, Tessa, is there a nice chestnut cake waiting for our supper? I am so hungry."

The boy's great black eyes sparkled as he told the story. His long hair hung down over his shoulders, under the odd pointed hat. He was a beautiful child. It was no wonder the American artist wished to put him in a picture.

But Tessa was beautiful, too. The artist would not be disappointed when he saw her. Her skin was clear, but like the colour of the olives which grew on the old tree behind her house. And now there was a faint pink blush in her cheeks as she listened to Beppo's story.

They were very happy children, but oh, so poor, you would think if you should visit them in the old house where they have always lived. It is no wonder they like best to be outdoors.

The house is all of stone, and the floor is made of bricks. It seems dark and chilly inside after leaving the glorious sunset. The plaster is blackened with smoke and age. In some places it is broken away from the wall and is falling down.

But there is a picture of the Christ-child hanging over the rough table, and the children do not think of the dingy walls. It is home, where a loving father and mother watch over them and guard them from harm.

See! the table is spread with the simple supper. There are the cakes made from chestnut flour mixed with olive oil, and of which Beppo is so fond. And here is milk from Tessa's pet goat. Beppo runs over to the stone fountain in the middle of the village and fills a copper dish with fresh water, and the little family sit down to their evening meal.

The mother hears the good news, and claps her hands in delight. But what shall Tessa wear? It troubles the good soul, for Tessa has no shoes, and both of her dresses are old and worn.

"Never mind, never mind," says her husband, "don't trouble yourself about that. The artist says he does not care about the clothes. He was much pleased with Beppo's cloak, however. He says it will be fine in the picture. Let Tessa wear her wide straw hat and her old clothes; that is all he asks."

"But how will she manage to travel so far? The child has never before gone such a distance from home," continued her mother.

"She is not heavy. She can sit on Pietro's back between the panniers. I will not load them heavily to-morrow, and then Pietro will not complain. And when we come home at night, Beppo can walk, I am sure. He may be tired, but he is a stout lad, my Beppo is. What do you say, my boy?"

Beppo was sure he could get along. He was only too glad to have Tessa's company.

"But think, babbo," he exclaimed, "it is not for one day that the artist wishes us. It is many, many, before the picture will be finished. We can manage somehow, I am sure. I am nearly twelve years old now, and I am getting very strong."

"But what will mother do with me away all day long?" said Tessa. "Who will take care of the baby while she works in the garden? And who will help her pull the weeds?"

"Bruno shall watch Francesca. He will let no harm come to her, you may be sure. Besides, she can walk alone so well now, she is little care. As for the garden, there is not much more to do at present. It almost takes care of itself," said the mother.

"Yes, Bruno can be trusted," said the father, "he is the best dog I ever knew."

As he heard his name spoken, the sheep-dog came slowly out of the chimney-corner. He wagged his tail as though he knew what his master and mistress had been saying. Beppo threw him his last bit of cake and Bruno caught it on his nose, from which it was quickly passed into his mouth.

"Dear old Bruno," said Tessa, "you took care of me when I was a baby, didn't you? Mamma, did Bruno really rock the cradle and keep the flies off, so I could sleep?"

"Yes, my child; when I was very ill he would watch you all day long. And when you began to creep, he followed you about. If you got near the edge of a step, or any other unsafe place, he would lift you by your dress and bring you to my side. We should thank the good Lord for bringing Bruno to us."

The mother looked up to the picture of Jesus and made the sign of the cross on her breast.

An hour later the whole family were sound asleep on their hard beds.

CHAPTER II

ROME

About four o'clock the next morning every one was awake and stirring. There was much to be done. The vegetables and fruits must be gathered; the donkey fed and saddled; Tessa's hair must be carefully combed and arranged in two long braids, and the breakfast of hard bread and olives eaten.

Tessa could not eat as much as usual to-day, she was so greatly excited. Think of it! This was to be her first trip to the great city. Her father and Beppo had told her so much about the wonderful sights there, and now she was going to look at them with her own eyes. Perhaps she would see the children of the artist. Beppo had told her of their blue eyes and golden hair. He called them little angels.

Donkey being led by man with two children "BEPPO WALKED BY HER SIDE"
Ah! she would like to be fair like them, she thought, as she looked in her tiny mirror. She did not dream how they would admire her own sweet dark face and soft voice.

Now it was six o'clock and time to start. Tessa seated herself on Pietro's back with her legs hidden by the bags of fruit. Beppo walked by her side, while her father went ahead leading Pietro by a rope.

Although it was so early, everybody in the village seemed to be up and doing. As she passed along, Tessa nodded good morning to the old women knitting or braiding straw on the door-steps.

"Pietro, do be careful," she cried, as the donkey picked his way among babies tumbling over each other in the narrow street while the older children played about them.

Our little party passed the fountain where a group of women were doing the family washing. Every one had a good word for Tessa, and wished her well, for the good news of last night had travelled from house to house.

The narrow streets were paved with blocks of black lava which had once flowed red-hot from the volcano, Vesuvius. High stone buildings that were hundreds of years old stood on each side. Perhaps in far-away times they had been forts or castles, but now the simple peasants lived in them with no thought of the grand old days of their country.

For this was Italy, the land of sunny skies and the treasure-house of the world. Look in your geography at the map of Europe and find the oddly shaped peninsula that stretches downward between two seas. It looks something like a man's boot, don't you think so?

Tessa doesn't know anything about the shape of her country, however. She has never studied geography. In fact, she can't even read, for she has been to school only six months altogether.

The good priest in the village loves the little girl. He has known Beppo and Tessa ever since they were born. He has tried to make it possible for these children to get learning, but many things have happened to prevent their studying.

One winter their father had a broken leg; at another, their mother was sick in bed for one whole year. When that trouble was over, the chestnut crop was very poor, and every one in the family had to work hard to earn enough to save them from starving. Something had been the matter nearly all the time, yet they had kept cheerful and happy. A change would come at last, if they loved the good Lord as they should. This is what Tessa's mother had said again and again.

The little girl thought of her mother's words as she rode proudly off on the donkey.

One of Beppo's boy friends went with them as far as the pasture-land below the village. He was driving a flock of goats which he must tend during the day. It was an easy life, but very tedious, and the boy wished he could go to the city, too. He had been there once, to the carnival. It was the grand time of his life, and he loved to tell the story over and over to his young friends.

At first the donkey trotted along quite merrily. His feet were so sure that Tessa had no fear of his stumbling, though the way at first was steep and stony.

"Good Pietro," said his little rider as she patted his head.

Perhaps the praise was too much for him, for Pietro turned his head to one side and came to a standstill. An idea seemed to have come to him. It was time for rest and a lunch. Look at those nice tufts of grass by the roadside. They must not be left behind. And Pietro began to nibble, as though he had no idea of the important business of the day.

Tessa coaxed and Beppo scolded, but the donkey would not budge. It was only when his master turned back and snapped the whip, that he changed his mind about going forward.

This was only the first of many such stops before they drew near the city that was once the greatest in the whole world. It well deserved the name of Rome, or "The Famous."

"What are those large mounds we are passing?" Tessa asked her father as she looked off over the Campagna.

"Those are tombs of men who lived ages ago in this loved country of ours. They were very great, and did noble deeds."

"But, babbo, there is a house built on one of the mounds."

"Yes, my child, the people have not kept them honoured as they should."

"Tessa, look at that stone water-way running through the plain," said Beppo. "They have told me in the city that a great ruler built it thousands of years ago. Think of that, Tessa. Thousands! It cost vast sums of money, and was made to bring the water to the city from the distant mountains. In those days great quantities of water were used in immense bath-houses. But see, we are passing an inn. I wish we were rich enough to go in and have some lunch."

His father heard Beppo's words. "Don't wish for what you cannot have, my boy," he said. "Look at that poor old man tending his flock of sheep, and be glad you are young and gay. That is best of all."

The Italians dread old age, and many of the peasants fear death. Beppo saw the shadow pass across his father's face, and, like a good son, tried to make it look as cheerful as usual.

"You shall not grow old and bent like that, babbo. Tessa and I will soon be able to let you take your ease. What do you say, sister?"

Tessa laughed, and answered, "Oh, yes, babbo, your work is nearly done now, for we are fast growing up."

Tessa was only nine years old, but coming to the city to be a model made her feel as though she were a young woman already. They now entered the wonderful city filled with treasures.

It disappointed Tessa at first. The streets were narrow and crooked, like those of her own little village. The high stone houses looked dark and gloomy. And there were beggars here! They looked poorer and more ragged than any people at home. Here was an old blind woman holding out a plate in which the passers-by were asked to put a piece of money. Tessa wished she could help her, but she was too poor herself, and the party passed on.

"You can't tell about these places by the outside," Beppo whispered. "Many of them are palaces, Tessa. Just wait till we come to our artist's house. It is grand inside, and there is a court in the middle of the building with fountains and statues and beautiful plants. And back of the house—but I won't tell you any more. You must wait till you get there. It is very lovely."

At last the donkey came to a standstill in front of a tall building. It was seven stories high and was all of marble.

"You knew when to stop, little beastie," said his master. "You never make mistakes of that kind, if you do like to nibble the grass at the wrong time. Get down, Tessa, this is where Mr. Gray lives.

"The artist has his studio far up at the top of the building. You are to go there this morning, but his family live on the fourth piano. Good-bye, little ones. Be good children." The father kissed them lovingly and went away with Pietro to sell his fruit.

Piano, as applied to a building, means floor in Italian. It is very common in Italy to find very different kinds of people living on the several floors, or pianos, of one building. In this old palace, which Tessa and Beppo entered for the first time, very poor and dirty families were huddled together on the first floor with their dogs and other pets. Yes, even the horse of one of the families shared their home in this fine building.

But overhead, on the second floor, there lived a prince, a real live prince, with a dozen servants to wait on him. It did not trouble him that poor and dirty people were below him, because the walls were high and thick, and the floors were of marble. He did not seem to know even that there were such people in the world.

Beppo and Tessa climbed twenty-seven marble steps before they came to the second piano; and still they must keep going up, up, up, until they reached the very top.

"Stop, stop," Tessa had to say more than once. "I am quite out of breath, and then, too, I am scared just a little bit. Beppo, do I look all right? Do you think the artist will take me?"

Then Beppo would put his arm around his sister and comfort her with loving words. But at last the studio was reached, and the children, flushed and excited, knocked at the door.

"My father came with us to the city to-day. He said you wished to see us," Beppo grew bold enough to say when a pleasant-faced gentleman opened the door. "He will call for us again to-night."

"Come in, little ones," the gentleman answered in Italian. "I am glad you are here. This is Beppo, I believe. I have seen you before. And here is the little sister. How do you do, my child? Make yourselves quite at home in these easy chairs."

While he was speaking to the children he was thinking, "How beautiful the little girl is! She will do finely. The two will make a great picture. My own children must see them."

Then he went on talking with Tessa. He showed her some curiosities and she soon forgot her bashfulness. But it was a long day. To be sure, the children had a delicious lunch which a servant brought up to the studio. The kind artist insisted they should not touch the food they had brought with them from home.

But after all, it was very tiresome to sit quite still for half an hour at a time. And all the while the strange gentleman's eyes were fixed on them while his hand was busy with the brush.

"This is just a sketch to-day, children. After this, I shall need only one of you at a time. But I like to have you come together, nevertheless. And now your work is over for the day.

"Pretty hard not to move about freely, little one, isn't it?" he said, as he patted Tessa on the chin. Then he rang the bell and told the servant to call his own children up to the studio. He would not have done this if he had not seen that his young models were unlike many of the poor children of the city.

"They are gentle and polite, if they are peasants," he said to himself. "My wife will be pleased, for Lucy and Arthur are lonesome and need some playmates of their own age."

A moment afterward merry voices were heard and the Gray children came skipping into the room.

"They are certainly angels," Tessa said to herself when she saw the golden curls of Lucy and the fair, sweet faces of her brother and herself. But she could not tell what they said, for they spoke in a strange tongue.

"It is not soft like our own dear Italian," she whispered to Beppo. "It is hard, this American language."

"They call it English, and not American," her brother answered. "I am going to learn it sometime, myself."

The artist turned from them to his own children. He spoke in Italian. "Lucy and Arthur are just beginning to speak your tongue, Tessa, but they learn fast.

They wish to know you and Beppo. I told them you were coming. They would like to play with you, but as yet they cannot talk much Italian. It is an hour yet before your father will come for you. Would you like to go down into the garden and walk among the flowers for a little while?"

Tessa's eyes sparkled with delight, and her heart beat quite fast when Lucy stretched out her white hand and held fast her own brown one.

"Come, Tessa and Beppo," said Arthur, who now spoke to his young visitors for the first time. "Come, and I will show you the garden."

The four children left the studio and ran down the great staircase. They did not stop until they found themselves on the ground floor. Then they passed out through a wide doorway into the courtyard.

Tessa held her breath with delight.

"Beppo, Beppo, look at that fountain," she cried. "And see the lovely cherub with its wings spread."

Lucy understood the words and she was pleased.

"The prince owns this court," she said, "but he has told father that we may come here and bring our friends when we like. Let us go into the gardens beyond."

staircase and gardens with palace in background IN THE PALACE GARDEN
The little Italians had hardly time to notice the statues and the beautiful plants before they were led into the great garden.

Here were orange-trees loaded with the yellow fruit. There were beds of flowers in bloom, although it was late in November. Beyond, were stone walls over which delicate vines were creeping, and marble statues were half hidden in the niches.

"There is a lizard," cried Arthur. "Don't you see him creeping along that stone wall? He's a little fellow, but, oh, my, he's quick in his motions."

"Listen!" said Beppo, who had forgotten his shyness now. "I will charm him. But you must all keep still."

He gave a long, low whistle. The lizard, which had crept into a hole, raised his head and looked toward the children in delight, as he drew himself to the top of the wall and lay quite still.

Again Beppo whistled in the same way, and the lizard crept nearer. And now he stretched himself at length upon the walk at Beppo's feet.

"I could keep him charmed like that all day long," said the boy. "It is queer, isn't it? Did you ever notice a lizard's feet?"

"What do you mean? The odd way the toes swell out on the edges?" Arthur asked.

"Yes. That is why the creature can walk across the ceiling like a fly. But it isn't the only reason, for a sticky substance oozes out, and that helps his feet to fasten themselves. I've seen them do it many times."

"I wonder how they make that queer noise," said Lucy.

"They smack their tongues back in their mouths, somehow," answered Beppo. "They are ugly little things, aren't they? But mother won't let me kill them when they get in the house, because they eat up the flies and spiders."

The children were walking now between two rows of laurel-trees.

"How dark and glossy the leaves are," said Lucy. "I think they are lovely. I like to get them and make wreaths. Then I take them up-stairs and put them on father's and mother's heads. I pretend I am crowning them as the heroes in Italy were crowned long ago." Lucy forgot her Italian and fell into English before she had half finished. It was no wonder that Tessa and Beppo could not understand.

Arthur saw the puzzled look in their faces and tried to explain. He was older than his sister and could speak Italian better than she.

"Lucy means this: I suppose you know that your country was once very great."

Beppo nodded his head. Oh, yes, and he believed it to be very great, still.

"And Rome was the leading city in the whole wide world," Arthur went on. "Great deeds were done by her people; great battles were fought; great books were written; great palaces were built. Well, in the olden times, whenever a person had done some truly great thing, he was crowned with a wreath of laurels. Father told me this, so I know it must be true.

"But come, I am afraid your father will be waiting for you. I didn't notice how fast the time was going."

They hurried back to the house. There, to be sure, were Pietro and his master. It had been a fine day. The fruit was all sold for a good price, and their father was eager to hear how the time had passed with his children.

"Oh, babbo, babbo, they were so kind, those good Americans. And I am very happy," said Tessa. She said this softly as she leaned over the donkey's side to pat her father's face while they were on the way home.

"The little girl (her name is Lucy, babbo,) did not seem to notice my bare feet and darned frock. She held my hand a long time, and I know I shall love her."

CHAPTER III

THE STORY OF ÆNEAS

Day after day Tessa and Beppo travelled over the road to Rome with their father. They were always happy, always gentle, always merry.

The artist and his family grew to love the children and wish they could do something to make their lives easier.

"They are so poor," Lucy told her brother one night, "that they eat meat only at great times, like Christmas. It costs too much for them to buy it every day as mother does. But they have plenty of fruit. I think the delicious figs and apricots that grow here in this country make up for a good deal of meat. And their mother makes salads of all kinds of vegetables. Perhaps they don't miss the meat as long as they are not used to eating it as we are."

"How did you know about their food?" asked Lucy's mother, who happened to hear what she said.

"It came about this way, mamma. We were in the kitchen the other day. I wanted to watch the maid cooking over the charcoal flames in that queer stone stove. And Tessa said then she had seen such a big piece of meat roasting for dinner only two or three times in her life. Then we went on talking and she spoke of what she usually had at home. Her mother uses olive oil in almost everything, just as our cook does. I should think it would be better than the lard we have in America, isn't it?"

"Yes, indeed, for it is much more wholesome. It is obtained from olives, you know, instead of the fat of pigs. People would use more of it in America if it did not cost so much by the time it has travelled across the ocean. But I hear your father's footsteps. Let us go and meet him."

The artist was not alone, for Tessa was with him. She was looking much pleased.

"It is raining hard," said Mr. Gray, "and I have just seen Tessa's father and asked him to let her spend the night with us. It is too great a storm for her to go out in. The little girl has done finely for me to-day, and she sat so well that I got along on my picture quite rapidly. So she will dine with us to-night and I will tell you stories in Italian. After that, we will have games."

Lucy ran and put her arms around Tessa's neck.

"What a good time we shall have," she cried. "Father tells lovely stories. Oh, Tessa, I wish you were my own sister."

Tessa turned her big dark eyes to the floor. There were tears in them, but they were tears of gladness. She had never had a cross word spoken to her in her whole life. She had never been punished for any little fault. But her loving little heart had not expected this: that the American child who was always dressed so beautifully, whose parents seemed so rich in her eyes, should wish a sister like her, a peasant girl. She could scarcely believe it.

The dinner seemed a very grand one to Tessa. One surprise was brought in after another. There were four separate courses! Last, came a delicious ice and frosted cakes. It seemed to the little Italian like a feast of the fairies.

After the dinner was over, the family went into the great drawing-room. Rugs were stretched here and there over the marble floor. There were soft couches and odd, spider-legged tables and chairs.

"We don't own the furniture," Lucy told her visitor. "It belongs here in the palace and is the same kind as the prince uses. He lives below us. It is beautiful, father thinks, but he does wish we could be warmer on these cold, windy days. You have very queer stoves in your country, Tessa. You should feel the heat that comes from ours in America." And Lucy held her hands over the jar filled with burning charcoal. It certainly gave the room little extra warmth.

"You look cold," Tessa answered, with her voice full of sympathy. "I do not feel so, though. I suppose it is because I have lived out-of-doors most of my life. But think, we do not have much weather like this, and it will soon be spring."

Yes, it was true. Christmas would be here in a few days, and then, then, the lovely spring would open with its violets, its daisies, and its strawberries.

"Are you ready with your story, father?" asked Lucy, as she perched herself on the arm of his chair. Arthur stretched himself on a rug at his father's feet, and at the same time drew Tessa on her low stool to his side.

"I shall have to be ready, at any rate, I think," her father answered, laughing. "So prepare to listen closely, for I must speak in Italian, that Tessa may understand.

"I wish you to imagine a time of long ago," he went on. "It was before any history was written about this country. There were many different tribes of people who lived along the shores of the rivers and built temples to strange gods. Those people believed in a god of the forest, and others of the ocean, the fruits, and the grains. Festivals were held in their honour.

"After many years, the country became great and powerful. This city was built and ships were sent from it to all parts of the known world. It was at this time also that art and poetry flourished. Sculptors modelled beautiful statues that we count among our greatest treasures to-day. And men wrote great books that you, Lucy and Arthur, will study, by and by.

"One of these writers was Virgil. He wrote in Latin, the language spoken by these people. The soft Italian words in use now are pleasant to the ear, but not as strong and grand as the old Latin tongue."

"Doesn't any one speak in Latin now, father?" asked Lucy.

"No, my dear. But it is studied, and the books written in Latin are read by scholars. Our own English language would be very poor if it had not received a great deal of help from the Latin. In fact, the same thing can be said of nearly every language used in the Western world to-day. But I am afraid you are getting tired. I will go back to my story.

"It was written by the poet Virgil, and tells of the wonderful things that happened to a prince called Æneas. He lived in Troy and was always called the Pious Æneas. This was because he was so good to his old father, and honoured the gods in whom he believed."

"Did he really live, father, or is this only a legend?" asked Arthur.

"We think now it is a legend, but the story is written as if every word were true, and belonged to the real history of Italy. But let me go on with my story.

"Æneas and his people had been conquered in a great battle, and their city was given up to their enemies. The young prince fled in the darkness, carrying his father on his back, and leading his little boy by the hand. His wife followed behind them. The old man carefully held some little images. They must not be left behind or lost, for they represented the gods in whom the Trojans believed and whom they worshipped.

"When they had gone a little way, Æneas found that his wife was no longer following them. What could have happened to her? He looked for her everywhere, but it was of no use. No trace of her could be found, and she was never heard of again.

"When Æneas and his men reached Mount Ida they built some ships and set sail. They would find a new home for themselves."

"But where was their old home, father? You called it Troy," said Lucy.

"Troy was a place in Asia Minor, near the strait with the long name of the Hellespont. This strait separates that part of Asia from Greece, and the rest of Europe. You can easily find it on your map. But remember this, as I go on,—in olden times the ships were small and people knew little about the seas or the great ocean, and seldom went far from home. What you would think of as a short voyage would have seemed a very long one to the people then.

"Many wonderful things happened to Æneas after he left Troy. After a while his provisions gave out, and he landed on the shore of an island to get some food. He found wild goats grazing there, and his men killed some of them. While they were feasting on the flesh of these creatures, the harpies appeared. They had the bodies of birds, but the faces of ugly old women."

Tessa shuddered. "Are there any real harpies?" she asked, eagerly.

"No, no, Tessa. Remember that this is only a legend.

"These horrible bird-hags flew down into the midst of the Trojans and destroyed their dinner. The men shot at them, but the arrows glanced off of the feathers, and not one of the harpies was harmed. Although most of them flew far away, they were very angry. One of them stayed long enough to cry in a harsh voice:

"'You Trojans shall be punished for troubling us. You shall be tossed about on the ocean until you reach Italy, and you shall not build a city for yourselves until you are so hungry that you will be willing to eat the trenchers containing the food.'

"This was what people called a prophecy, and, as Æneas and his men believed in such things, it made them feel far from cheerful.

"He sailed away, however, and came at length to another place, where he found old friends. His cousin, Helenus, who had also been driven away from Troy, was ruling there, and he had built a new city for himself and his comrades.

"Helenus was a prophet, as it seemed, and he told Æneas that after he reached Italy he would find an old white sow with thirty little pigs around her. He must build a city for himself wherever he should find her.

"Æneas had many other adventures after leaving Helenus. Among other things, he met a horrible giant who had lost the sight of his one eye, but was still terrible. After this, the old father of Æneas died, and the son's sad loss was followed by a fearful storm in which the men nearly gave up hope of seeing land again. The ships were driven far to the south.

"After the wind had died down and the waves had grown calmer, the homeless wanderers came to a quiet bay. They landed and found a lovely queen who treated Æneas so kindly that he almost forgot the city he had planned to build in Italy. But after awhile the god Mercury appeared to him and reminded him of his duty.

"He set sail once more, leaving the beautiful queen so unhappy that she killed herself with a sword her visitor had left behind. There were many other adventures, but, at last, Æneas came to the shores of Italy, where he rested in a grove. He and his followers sat around on the grass to eat. They used large, round cakes for plates on which to place the meat. After it was gone, they began to eat the cakes. Then Æneas's little son said:

"'We are eating our trenchers.'

"When he heard these words Æneas thought of the harpy's prophecy. He knew at once that his home was to be here."

"Was it where Rome stands now?" asked Lucy.

"No, the place was called Cumæ. There is another story about the building of Rome which you may like to hear some other evening. Let us play games for awhile, and then, little ones, for bed and pleasant dreams."

Every one joined in a game of blind man's buff. Tessa had never played it before and she enjoyed it very much. Then she showed them how to play one of the games she had learned from the children of her own village.

CHAPTER IV

CHRISTMAS

"Mother," said Lucy, one day late in December, "Tessa says she never gets presents on Christmas Day. Those always come on Twelfth Night in Italy. What a queer idea! But she says there are processions in the churches, and all sorts of beautiful sights. Will father take us to Saint Peter's then, do you think?"

Lucy had only been in Italy six months and there were many interesting things she had not seen yet.

"Certainly," answered her mother. "Your father and I have been thinking of asking both Tessa and Beppo to spend Christmas week with us. You will enjoy the sights all the more if you have them with you. What do you think?"

Lucy was so pleased she jumped up and down in delight.

"You good, kind mother," she cried. "Of course, it will be lovely."

That very night Tessa's father was asked if he would be willing his children should visit the artist's family. The good man's face beamed with pride. Oh, yes, he was only too glad they should have such an honour and pleasure. He knew his wife would also rejoice.

There was to be no trouble about the clothes. A new suit was already waiting for Beppo, while the artist's wife had herself made two pretty dresses for Tessa.

"You are too kind," cried the peasant. His hands seemed to say this as well as his voice. What would an Italian do without hands to help him in talking? Sometimes they seem to express more than his voice.

In this way it came to pass that Tessa and Beppo bade good-bye to the little village on the hillside for nearly two weeks. They must be home at Twelfth Night, however, to bring presents to mother and Francesca. Oh, yes, there was no doubt of that.

But in the meantime it was to be a holiday. The children were not to sit as models for one minute. The artist would let his brushes rest and go about the city with his family and their young visitors.

Christmas Eve came at last, although the hours before it arrived seemed like weeks to the excited children.

A carriage drove up to the palace door. They were all to drive to a beautiful church called Santa Maria Maggiore, where the Pope himself would be that night.

"Why is he such a great man, and why do the people give him such reverence?" asked Arthur.

Tessa heard the question. Her pretty face flushed. "Why, Arthur, he is the head of our church, the Catholic Church," she answered, quickly. "It is not only here in Italy, but all over the world that we Catholics honour him!"

The little girl was ignorant about many things in her own city that Lucy and Arthur could explain to her, but she had been taught from birth to think of the Pope as the most holy person in the world.

But why was the Pope to be present in the church Christmas Eve? The children had already been told that on this occasion a piece of the cradle in which Jesus had lain was to be carried through the church. At least, Tessa and her brother and all good Catholics believed it to be a part of his cradle. They thought that by some miracle it had been saved for nineteen hundred years, and was now cared for sacredly in their loved city. Any one who wished, might look upon it at Christmas time.

The peasant children believed it could do great wonders. Why, if they were sick, and even dying, it might save their lives if they were allowed to touch it.

Tessa whispered this to Lucy as they mixed with the people entering the church. They passed along between two rows of beautiful marble columns. They were obliged to move slowly because the crowd was so great. But Lucy's father soon led them to the doorway of a small chapel, where they could stand while the procession passed up to the altar. The sacred cradle was carried first, and behind it followed the Pope with the cardinals and other high officers of the church.

The Pope was carried in a chair above the heads of the people and, as he passed along, he held out his hands to bless them as they knelt before him.

Tessa and Beppo had never looked upon him before. Indeed, they were scarcely able to see him or any other part of the procession now, because of the great crowd. But they knew he was there and that they were near him. This was enough to satisfy their pious little hearts. Lucy and Arthur were most pleased to think that these Italian friends were made so happy.

"Is that all, father?" Lucy whispered. "It is hot and close here. Can't we go home now and have our Christmas tree?"

Her father said that he was quite willing to go, for he saw that his wife was as tired as his little daughter.

An hour afterward they were in the great drawing-room at home. Many candles gave a soft and pleasant light to the room; for gas and electricity were not used in many Roman houses.

A curtain was drawn, and there stood a beautiful Christmas tree,—not of pine or balsam, such as Lucy and Arthur would have in America. It was of laurel.

"Oh! Oh! Oh!" exclaimed Beppo. He had never seen anything like it before, for his people are not used to this custom of having Christmas trees. And Tessa's eyes sparkled, too, as she drew one long sigh of happiness. What beauty met her eyes! Was it indeed fairy-land,—these tiny lights shining on every twig of the tree; gilded oranges hanging from the branches; and toys, so many she was sure she could not count them.

Could it be true that this lovely wax doll was her very own? Lucy's father had said so, but she was afraid she might rub her eyes and wake, and find it all a dream.

As for Beppo, he was equally delighted to find himself the owner of a jack-knife with four blades, a fine ball with which he could teach the American children his favourite game of pallone, in which he was very skilful.

There were neither skates nor sleds. They would be of no use in Italy, the land of sunny skies, where snow is unknown except on the high mountain-tops.

The evening was a merry one, but it came to an end at last.

"To bed, to bed, children," Lucy's mother cried at length. "To-morrow there will be more sights, and you must not get sick over your good time."

Christmas morning dawned bright and clear.

The children waked early and did not seem any the worse for sitting up so late the night before. Soon after breakfast, an open carriage appeared at the door of the palace and they all rode off to visit the greatest church in the world.

"At last we are on our way to Saint Peter's," said Arthur. "Tessa, you may well be proud when you think of the people who come here from all parts of the world to see the grand buildings."

Tessa was proud. This was her Italy, her Rome, her Saint Peter's. She, a poor little peasant maiden, felt richer at this moment than the owner of a million dollars.

The party had to ride over a bridge before they could reach the church.

"Do you know the name of the river over which this bridge is built?" Arthur asked his sister.

"The Tiber, the yellow Tiber," she answered gaily. "You ought to remember, Arthur, that father read us the poem a few days ago about the guarding of the bridge. It made a shiver creep down my back when I thought of the three men holding the bridge against the army of their enemies. It stretched across this very river."

"It was hundreds of years ago," Lucy went on, turning toward Tessa, "that those brave men saved the city. They kept the enemy from entering until the bridge was cut down. The last one stood on guard until he felt the supports give way. Then he cried out to the river:

"'O Tiber, Father Tiber, to whom the Romans pray,
A Roman's life, a Roman's arms take thou in charge this day.'
"An instant afterward he jumped into the rushing stream and swam with all his might back to his people and the city he had saved."

"Did he escape?" Beppo asked. "I should think his enemies would have killed him before he was able to get out of the reach of their weapons."

"They admired his bravery so much they had mercy on him and did not try to hit him after he jumped into the water. Then they turned away, for they could not reach Rome now that the bridge was destroyed."

As Lucy finished the story she could not help saying to herself, "I do hope Tessa and Beppo will be able to go to school and study about this grand country of theirs. They love it as dearly as I love America, but they do not know as much of the history of its great men as I do now."

Her father was thinking at the same time, "What a pity it is there are so many poor and ignorant people in Italy. How I wish the children of to-day could grow up and make the country what it was once."

The sun was shining so brightly by this time that the girls had to raise their parasols to shade their eyes as they looked along the crowded street. It was filled with carriages all going in the same direction as themselves. The sidewalks, too, were packed closely. There were all kinds of people; lords and ladies, priests in their shovel hats, cardinals in their elegant robes. All would soon enter the great church. Their faces looked happy and full of joy.

"Shall we not be crowded worse than we were last night?" asked Mrs. Gray. She looked a little bit worried.

"O no, you need have no fear about that," her husband replied. "Forty thousand people can easily gather in Saint Peter's and then it will not be full, by any means."

The carriage stopped in front of a long covered archway built of marble. They stepped down and, entering it, soon found themselves in the court in front of the church.

The church itself is built in the shape of an immense cross, and where the four lines of the cross meet, there is a huge dome overhead.

"I can see the dome of Saint Peter's from my home on the mountain," Tessa said to Lucy. "If I were far away in another part of the world, I am sure I should picture it in my mind whenever I thought of Rome."

CHAPTER V

SAINT PETER'S

The children now entered the great building. What a glory of colour was around them. There was a blaze of gold and purple and crimson. The windows were set with glass of all the beautiful tints of the rainbow. The floors were laid in small pieces of marble in exquisite patterns.

"Oh, Lucy, Lucy," whispered Tessa, "look at the walls and pillars! Gems such as your mother wears are shining there. And how beautifully they are carved."

Lucy's only answer was, "Look overhead, Tessa, and see the paintings. There are the figures of the apostles. They appear as large as life, although we are so far below them."

inside cathedral IN ST. PETER'S
 Just then her father told her to notice the pen in St. Luke's hand.

"I have been told that it is seven feet in length," he said, "yet it is so far away it seems only as long as the one you use at home, Lucy."

Soft music was now heard pealing from the organ, and they moved slowly along to the seats Mr. Gray had engaged for them.

"Look, look, Lucy!" whispered Tessa, a few minutes after. "He is coming, and we can see him to-day, I am sure."

It was the Pope, of course. Two enormous fans could be seen waving at the other end of the great building. The procession of priests and cardinals, in their purple robes, moved slowly and grandly along. The Pope was behind them in a chair carried on poles by twelve bearers. The fans were kept waving on each side of the great man.

As he passed onward between the rows of soldiers in their gorgeous uniforms, they knelt before him.

"He holds out only two fingers of his hand over the bent heads of the people. That is all there is of the blessing, I suppose," said Arthur. "But he smiles pleasantly, and has a kind face."

28

At last the procession reached the altar. The Pope stood up before the people, and they could see he was robed in white. He chanted the service, after which a choir of beautiful voices began to sing. The balcony where the singers stood was richly gilded.

When the service was ended, Mr. Gray told the children to wait quietly where they were.

"When most of the people have passed out," he said, "we will walk about and examine this beautiful cathedral more carefully. There is a great deal you have not seen yet."

In a few minutes the building was nearly empty, and Mr. Gray led the way from one part of it to another. He opened the door into one of the chapels at the side.

"Look within," he said. "This chapel is as large as an ordinary church. Yet there are a number just like it which lead from the main part of the cathedral. They seem tiny beside it, though."

Tessa and Beppo loved to stop at the different shrines where the figures of Jesus and his mother, Mary, were always found. They were beautifully carved and sparkled with rich jewels.

"Now let us visit the statue of St. Peter himself," said Mr. Gray. "Some say it was never meant for that good man, but is really the likeness of a heathen emperor. But nearly every one who worships here does not wish to believe that. And so many visitors have come here to give him honour that one toe of the statue is a good deal worn off."

"Why, what do you mean, father?" asked Lucy.

"Just what I said, my dear. It is thought to be quite proper to kiss the toe of the statue of St. Peter. I don't know how the fashion started, but, at any rate, I believe thousands upon thousands of people have knelt before the statue and done that very thing. You can see the marks of it for yourself."

After St. Peter had been duly examined, Mr. Gray proposed that a visit should be made to the wonderful dome.

"But there are a good many stairs to climb. Do you think, wife, that you will be able to mount them?"

"If the little girls can do it, I am sure that I can," replied Mrs. Gray, as she turned to Tessa and Lucy. It was quite easy to see by their smiles and nods that they were eager to try it.

"Then let us start at once," said her husband, beckoning to a guide to show the way.

They passed through a door in the side of the church, and entered a passage which wound round and round, yet up and still up, till they reached a balcony around the foot of the dome. The stairway by which they had come was so broad and rose so gradually that one could easily mount it on horseback.

"Many a person has ridden to the top on a donkey," the guide told the children, which amused them very much.

As they looked down from the balcony, the people in the body of the church seemed like tiny dolls, they were so far below.

"But this is not all," said Mr. Gray. "As soon as you stop panting, we will go higher yet."

"All ready, father," said Lucy, after a five minutes' rest. "I'm sure we are equal to another climb now."

The next flight of stairs was very narrow. It led to another balcony around the top of the dome.

"Do not think this is all," said Mr. Gray. "We can go higher yet, for we have not reached the lantern."

After much puffing and gasping for breath, and the climbing of more narrow stairs, they found themselves in a large room inside the lantern. As they looked out of the windows in that lofty place, a wonderful view was spread before their eyes. Below was the square, and leading out from it were many archways with curved tops, like the one through which the children first entered the church. The palace of the Pope was at hand, with its wonderful library and art treasures.

Beyond, across the Tiber, lay the great city, with its palaces, fountains, temples, and the ruins of the greatest and finest buildings in the world; some of them two thousand years old.

"I can look far out upon the sea that Columbus first sailed," exclaimed Arthur. "Indeed, it seems as if I could almost see Spain, where he went to get help. You know the story of Columbus, don't you, Beppo?"

The Italian lad shook his head. No, but he wished to hear it. Would Arthur tell him the story some day?

Arthur said he would be glad to do so, for, although Columbus was an Italian, he felt that he belonged to America. Where would he be now, if Columbus had not discovered the new world? Who should say?

"Look straight down at the roof of the church below us," cried Lucy. "Did you ever hear of anything so odd? There is a little cottage! The idea of a house built on the roof of a church! What can be the reason for its being there?"

"It is only a room made for the workmen," said the guide. "They are busy all the time repairing the church in one part or another."

"Now let us go home and have the Christmas dinner," said Mr. Gray, after they had rested a few moments longer.

An hour afterward the children were gathered around the great dining-table. But there was no Christmas turkey in the middle. There was a dish of larks instead!

"Poor little birds," said Lucy. "It is too bad to kill tiny things like you, that we may have something nice to eat."

"What is the bird of your country, Beppo?" asked Arthur.

"I don't know, but I think it ought to be the nightingale," the little Italian answered. "Ah! I love to hear him, he sings so sweetly." The boy's face lighted up as he said this. "And what is the bird of America, Arthur?" he asked.

"The eagle has been chosen, but I think it ought to be the turkey, for my country gave that glorious fowl to the world."

Mr. and Mrs. Gray laughed at Arthur's words, but a moment after his father said:

"I quite agree with you, my boy. The turkey truly belongs to us, while the eagle is not only found in many other lands, but it has been the national emblem of several countries."

The Christmas holidays passed only too quickly, and the day before Twelfth Night soon arrived. The shops were full of things suitable for presents, and a great fair was held in the city, around which crowds of Italians were busy buying their gifts. Beppo and Tessa wandered up and down with their American friends.

They were perplexed as to what they should get for their dear ones at home. There were many things from which to choose. They felt as though they had quite a little fortune to spend, for Mr. Gray had given each of them what would be equal to a dollar in our money.

They had never had so much money before, and they turned from one thing to another before they finally decided upon a dress and a big gilt brooch for their mother, a new hat for their father, and little red kid shoes for Francesca.

"She never had any shoes in her life," Tessa told Lucy. "I never had any either, till your mother gave me these."

When the peasant called at the palace to take the children home, he brought great news.

"We have a new baby," he said. "It is a beautiful boy just a day old. And now we must have a christening as soon as Twelfth Night is over. We will ask the kind artist and his wife, as well as our own friends, to come."

CHAPTER VI

THE CHRISTENING

Tessa and Beppo were so eager to see the precious baby, they could hardly wait to get home. They were even a little cross with Pietro when he stopped to nibble choice bits of grass by the roadside. But what could a poor stupid donkey be expected to care about a baby only a day old?

Home was reached at last, however, and the children bounded into the dark room where their mother lay watching for them. A small basket cradle stood beside the curtained bed; in it was the sweetest, tiniest baby.

"He is sound asleep, mamma," said Tessa, after kissing her mother at least a dozen times. "How I wish he would wake."

"I do believe he looks like me, the darling little boy," she exclaimed, when the baby's eyes opened at last.

The kind neighbour who had come in to look after the family for a few days lifted the baby tenderly and placed him in Tessa's arms. He was so swaddled in clothes and blankets it didn't seem as though he could be hurt, even if the little girl should drop the precious bundle. But there was no fear of that. She was used to babies, and had taken almost all the care of Francesca since that little girl was a month old.

But where was Francesca now? The little tot was holding fast to her sister's dress. She wanted to be as near as possible to this wonderful new brother. When he began to cry, she said:

"Baby wants the candle; baby wants the candle." She thought he had already begun to notice things about the room, and was longing for the lighted candle. Everybody laughed.

"He is hungry; that is all, you foolish Francesca. You are only a baby yourself," said Beppo.

After the baby had been put back in the cradle, Tessa went to the bedside of her mother and told her of her lovely visit to the grand home of the Americans.

"To-morrow, when you are not so tired, I will tell you more about it. But after all home is the best place in the world. Now that I can look at you, I don't care if I can't see the procession to-morrow. Just think! babbo says that an image of the Holy Child is carried up and down the aisles of one of the churches. It is richly dressed in silks and jewels. After awhile it is placed on a stage with wax figures of the Virgin and Joseph and the Three Wise Men. There is even a manger there, and a big cow or ox. It must be very beautiful."

"When you are older, we will go together," said the mother, softly. "I went to Rome on Twelfth Day several times when I was younger. But many things have happened to prevent it lately." She sighed as she thought of the sickness and the hard work of the last few years.

All the next day Francesca was so happy with the bright red shoes that she did not need to be watched. Every one, except the dear mother lying quietly behind the snowy bed-curtains, was busy preparing for the christening.

A bright fire was kept burning, and the odour of onions and garlic filled the kitchen. There must be all sorts of nice dishes at the morrow's feast, and the good neighbour was cooking from morning till night.

Among other things, she prepared some wonderful cakes. Tessa thought they were among the greatest dainties in the world. There were olives and pistachio-nuts and garlic in them, I am sure. Tessa would have to tell you the rest, for she helped in making them.

Every one was awake bright and early the next morning, and a crowd of the village people went with the father and baby to the little village church. Tessa and Beppo kept as near as possible to their new brother.

Mr. and Mrs. Gray, with Lucy and Arthur, arrived in a carriage just as the party was entering the church door. The children had begged so hard to come that their parents could not refuse.

Tessa and Lucy hugged and kissed each other as though they had been apart for a long time.

When all had entered the church, the baby was carried to the font and was baptized by the kind-faced priest.

What was his name now, you ask? It was Angelo, after his proud father, who handed him around among his friends as soon as the baptism was over. Every one must have a chance to kiss him. As he was passed from one to another, a piece of money was tucked away in his clothes by each one.

No matter how poor the person was, some little bit was given with a right good will. It was but a symbol of the love and friendship of these simple peasants for each other.

When Mr. Gray's turn came, he hid in the baby's dress a piece of money so big as to make his mother's eyes open with delight when it was shown her afterward. She had never before seen a gold coin worth ten dollars in her life.

The christening party now turned back to the house, where the mother lay waiting for them. The feast was all spread and the visitors gathered around the table with good appetites. Lucy and Arthur and their parents stayed, for Tessa's father looked quite hurt when they spoke of going home.

"Not stop to share our feast!" he cried. "Ah! that is sad! sad!"

And so they remained and took part in the merrymaking. Some of the villagers played on their bagpipes. Tessa performed a very pretty dance, and Beppo sang two songs with his rich, soft voice.

"We have had a lovely time," said Lucy, as the beautiful colours began to light the sunset sky, and her father bade her get ready to leave. "But we wish Tessa and Beppo to come home and stay with us another week. Don't we, father?"

Mr. Gray answered, "Yes, we should like it very much. After my holiday, I must paint quite steadily, and I wish to finish the picture of Tessa and Beppo at once. It would not be easy for you to bring the children to me every day now that your wife is sick. So please let them go back with us."

This was how Tessa and Beppo came to go back to Rome with the family of the artist. The carriage was a little crowded, but no one cared. All were so busy laughing and talking that it seemed only a few minutes before they drew near the city gates.

"I believe it was not far from here that Agrippa told the people the fable so often repeated since that time."

The painter was looking out of the carriage over the Campagna.

"I wish I knew the exact spot," he said, half to himself.

"Tell us about it; do, please, father," said Lucy. "What was the fable, and who was Agrippa, and why did he come out on this dreary place to tell a story?"

"It was a long time ago; even long before the birth of Jesus," Mr. Gray replied. "It was when Rome was a powerful city. There were two great classes of the people,—the patricians, who were rich and owned most of the land, and the plebeians, who had little power and were mostly poor.

"The patricians ruled the city to suit themselves and did not treat the plebeians justly. At last, when they could not stand this unfair treatment any longer, they came together and marched out of the city.

"'We will claim our rights,' they said, and made ready to attack the patricians, who remained in Rome.

"It was a time of danger for the city, since there was a greater number of the poor than of the rich. What should be done? A very wise man named Agrippa was chosen to go out on the Campagna and reason with the plebeians. When he drew near to them, he said:

"'I have a fable which I wish to tell you. It is this:

"'Once upon a time all the limbs of a man's body became provoked because they had to work for the stomach. The legs and feet were obliged to carry it about; the hands had to get food for it; the mouth ate for it; the throat swallowed for it; the head thought for it; and so on. They said it was a shame they had to work so hard for that one organ. What use was it, indeed!

"'They agreed to do nothing more for it at all. They stopped their work, but, strange to say, they began to grow weak and helpless. At last they said to each other, "We shall all starve and die unless we go back to our old work. The stomach has seemed useless to us before, but now we see that we were mistaken."'

"After he had ended his story, Agrippa went on to say that all classes of people depended on each other, and that all would perish unless they worked together.

"Both the poor and the rich seemed to think that this was good advice. The plebeians marched back into the city and took up their old work, while the patricians promised to be fairer in their dealings.

"Thus peace was made and Rome was saved."

As Mr. Gray finished the story the carriage drew up in front of their home.

"What a short ride it seemed," said Tessa. "It must have been because of the story you told us, Mr. Gray. I shall never forget it."

CHAPTER VII

THE TWINS

"Tessa and Beppo are two of the best models I ever had," said Mr. Gray. "They were perfectly quiet and did just what I wished. My picture is finished and you must all come up and look at it."

It was a sunny afternoon nearly a week after the christening of Tessa's baby brother. Lucy and Arthur were in the drawing-room with their mother when Mr. Gray opened the door with these words.

There was a great scampering over the stairs as the two children tried to see who could reach the studio first.

"Oh, how lovely, how lovely!" cried Lucy, who was the winner of the race. She was standing in front of the canvas.

And what do you think she saw? A little flower-girl out on the Campagna. She sat on the back of a donkey that certainly looked much like Pietro. The girl's bare feet were almost hidden by two great bags of fruit hanging from the donkey's sides.

In her lap was a basket of flowers that she would sell in the city to-day. A boy who was the very image of Beppo held the donkey's bridle.

"How beautiful you have made Tessa's curls," said Lucy. "But they are not a bit lovelier than hers really are. Look at the feather in Beppo's pointed hat, Arthur, and the gaiters buttoned up to the knees. And see the brown cloak thrown over his shoulders. It's the very way he wears it."

"But you haven't noticed the herd of oxen in the distance," said the modest little Tessa. She was quite abashed by the attention given to the figures of her brother and herself. "They are going back to the hillside for the night. What a lovely soft gray they are painted. I love these dear gentle creatures. They could do great harm with their large, spreading horns, but they are too kind for that."

"Yes, and see the shepherds standing in that field of daisies," said Beppo. "More than once my father and I have stayed all night in just such a place when the storm overtook us and we could not get home."

"How I love the mountains, far away in the soft light," said Mrs. Gray. "They make a beautiful background for the rest of the picture."

"When you have admired it as much as you like, I think we had better take a half-holiday and see some of the sights," proposed Mr. Gray. "It is only two o'clock now; how soon can you all be ready?"

"In five minutes, can't we, mother?" said Lucy, who was always delighted to have her father's company. He was usually so busy he could not often go anywhere with them.

"Yes," said Mrs. Gray. "We will not delay. Get your hats, children; we can come here to-morrow to enjoy the picture again."

This time they decided to walk, that the children might stop wherever they wished.

"What is this show? Oh, do look!" cried Tessa, as they came to a big box set up on the side of the street. A man could be seen partly hidden behind the curtain. He was making some puppets act out a little play. He changed his voice so as to represent first one, then another.

"That is a Punch and Judy show," said Arthur. "You may watch it while I go over to that little flower-girl's stand. I am going to buy a bunch of pansies for mother. I think that is the girl's grandfather standing by her side. He must be lame, for he has a crutch. I suppose they are very poor. Perhaps that child supports them both."

After Arthur had bought his flowers, they walked on till they came to a shrine set up against the wall. It was a picture of Saint Mary and the infant Jesus in a rough wooden frame.

Tessa and Beppo knelt before it and were very quiet for a minute or two.

"They are repeating some prayers," whispered Lucy to her brother, as they passed slowly on. "When we rode back from Tessa's home the other night, I noticed she suddenly stopped talking and shut her eyes when we passed one of those shrines out on the Campagna."

"She is a good little Catholic."

"Arthur, look at that poor donkey. You can't see anything but his legs and his nose. He is carrying such a big load of hay that the rest of his body is out of sight."

Their father came up to them at this moment, and said: "How would you like to take a carriage now and visit the Coliseum? We still have plenty of time, and I have never been there with you."

"Good! good!" cried the children.

While they were waiting for the carriage they bought some of the big Italian chestnuts at a stand where a boy stood roasting them for the passers-by.

They had not ridden far before they came upon a crowd of people around a fire.

"What are they doing?" asked Lucy.

"I think I know," Tessa answered. "They are heating pine-cones so as to get the seeds. Did you ever eat them, Lucy? I am very fond of them."

"What a queer idea! But then, your pine-trees are different from any I have seen growing at home. I don't doubt they are very nice."

When they drove up in front of the Coliseum, they saw before them one of the grandest ruins in the world. It was built when Rome was still a great city, and was made to hold eighty thousand people.

"Why do you speak of it as a 'sacred ruin,' father?" asked Arthur.

"Whenever we look at it we think of the Christians who suffered terrible deaths there because of what they believed," Mr. Gray answered. "The Coliseum was finished about seventy years after the birth of Jesus. It was the place where the public games went on and where the wild beast shows and fights were held.

"You can see that one side of the great wall of the building is still standing in pretty good condition. It was made in the shape of an oval, as you also see. Now, imagine an open space, or arena, in the middle, and all around it rows on rows of seats, built one above the other.

"Listen! Can't you imagine you hear the roars of wild beasts that were once kept in vaults beneath the building? When they were needed they were drawn up in their cages into the arena.

"After the spectators had taken their seats, a signal was given and the doors of the cages were flung open. The furious beasts would rush out and frightful scenes would follow. The creatures were either set against each other or against men who had been sentenced to death."

"And would people go to see such terrible things for their own pleasure?" asked Tessa. Her face was full of pain at the idea.

"Yes, my dear. It showed that the city was in a bad state when the Romans could take delight in seeing other creatures suffer, whether they were men or beasts," was the answer.

"But I told you that we of to-day hold the place sacred to the Christians. That is because in those sad times they were cruelly put to death here. One good bishop, I remember, was killed by lions in this very spot. But he went to his death cheerfully,—he was glad to be a martyr to his faith."

"It looks bright and pleasant now," said Mrs. Gray. "It is hard to believe that such dreadful things ever took place here. See the pretty vines growing out between the stones in the wall; and listen to the shouts of those boys as they run and jump among the ruins."

As the children seemed ready for a change, Mr. Gray proposed that they should visit the Capitol, where they could see many beautiful statues; after which, they must go home, for the afternoon was nearly gone.

That evening Lucy took her place on one arm of her father's chair and told Tessa to take the other.

"Now, boys," said she, "stop talking and be quiet, and perhaps father won't be too tired to tell us about the building of Rome. Will you, father dear?"

Mr. Gray could never refuse his little daughter when she spoke like that. And if this had not been enough, there were Tessa's great soft eyes looking at him. They seemed to say, "Oh, do, please, tell us," although Tessa herself was too shy to ask him with her voice.

"About Rome, you say. All right.

"Once upon a time there were two little boys—"

"But when was this 'once upon a time?'" interrupted Arthur. "You began the story of Æneas with the very same words."

"It was quite a while after Æneas settled in Italy. The two boys were his great-great-great-grandchildren; thirteen times great, I believe. Their mother was a vestal virgin,—that is, she was a maiden who tended the sacred fire in the temple of the goddess Vesta. Such maidens were treated with great honour, but they were not allowed to marry.

"So the people were very angry when the young girl claimed that the god Mars was her husband, and that the two baby boys were his and her children. So the poor girl was buried alive, while the helpless babies were put in a trough and set afloat on the river Tiber."

"Poor little things! Were they drowned?" asked Beppo.

"No, for if they had been, there would be no more story to tell," said Mr. Gray.

"It happened that the river was very high at that time and had overflowed its banks, just as it sometimes does nowadays. The water settled down soon afterward and the two boys were left high and dry on the bank.

"And now what do you suppose came along and saw the children?"

"Some bad men," answered Arthur.

"The boys' mother, who had escaped from her grave," guessed Beppo.

"No. It was a mother wolf, who carried them home to her lair and fondled and nursed them," was the answer.

"After a while a shepherd discovered the babies with their adopted mother. He was a good man, with a kind heart, and took them home to his wife. She gave them the names Romulus and Remus, and brought them up to be shepherds like her husband."

"Oh, father, do you suppose all this was really true?" asked Lucy.

"No more than the story of Æneas. I think it is a legend handed down by the people for thousands of years. But listen, for I have not finished, and it spoils the story to be all the time wondering whether it is true or not.

"When the twin brothers grew up, they fought in a battle that took place between the shepherds of the boys' grandfather, who ought to have been king, and those of the wrongful ruler of the country.

"Romulus and Remus did such brave deeds that they were noticed and taken before their grandfather. After many questions, he discovered who they really were. They gathered an army together, and marching out to battle, seized the country in their grandfather's name.

"They must build a city now for themselves, they thought. They looked over the seven hills on which Rome now stands. They said the city must be on one of these hills, but which hill should it be? Romulus chose one, and Remus another. They could not agree. Their grandfather said, 'Watch for a sign from the gods.' So Romulus took his place on the hill he had chosen, and Remus on his.

"Remus was the first to see any sign from heaven. It was six vultures flying. But Romulus soon saw twelve of these birds, and so the right was given him to found the city on the Palatine Hill. The people chose him king.

"But Remus was angry. He thought he should have been given the right to found the city, as he had been the first to see birds.

"As the mud walls were being built around the place where the city was to stand, he leaped over them in scorn. His brother looked upon this as an insult, and killed him on the spot, saying, 'Every one who leaps over the walls of my city shall perish even as you do.'

"After this sad deed the work went on. Romulus marked out his city in the shape of a square. It is said that he did this with a plough. He said, 'I will call my city Rome.'

"He lived here in a hut made of mud, with a thatched roof.

"That was the beginning of this wonderful city, so the people will tell you."

Tessa nodded her head; she and Beppo had heard the story before, and fully believed it to be true.

"How long ago do they say all this happened, father?" asked Lucy.

"They claim that Rome was built years before the birth of Christ. If it is now , years since his birth, how many years old is Rome?"

"Let me see: and , are ,. It was , years ago. Whew! what a long time," said Arthur. "Many things have happened since then."

<h1 style="text-align:center">CHAPTER VIII</h1>

<h2 style="text-align:center">THE CARNIVAL</h2>

It was now February. Tessa and Beppo had been home for several weeks. The baby was growing fast; the mother was strong again and rosy; while the extra money which the children had earned as models for Mr. Gray had made the family very comfortable.

"How would you like to go to the carnival?" the father asked.

The family were gathered around the table where the dish of polenta had just been placed. Polenta, you must know, is a kind of porridge made of corn (maize) meal. It was the only food the children would have for supper that night. But that did not seem to trouble them. They all looked happy, even before they heard the word carnival.

But this had a wonderful effect. Tessa jumped up, caught the baby out of his cradle, and began to dance about the room. Beppo seized his violin and started a lively air. Their mother began to laugh, while little Francesca looked from one to another in surprise. She could not understand what the sudden excitement was about.

When Tessa had danced herself nearly out of breath, she ran and put her arms around her father's neck.

"Oh, babbo, babbo! do you really mean it?" she cried. "I have never been to the carnival, and I have heard so much about the beautiful festival."

Then her mother spoke. She blushed like a young girl as she said to her husband:

"It would seem like old times before we were married, to go to the gay carnival together. But how shall we manage it with our family of four children?"

45

"I have fixed all that," her husband answered. "We are to stay with your cousin Lola in the city. She will keep us through the week for a small sum, as she says she has an extra room that she will be glad to have us use.

"So get ready, wife, and look as fine as possible in your new blue skirt and the red bodice below the white blouse. Do not forget to wear the fringed kerchief on your pretty head. It is the one I gave you when you were a gay young girl."

His wife promised to make herself look as fine as possible, as she blushed more deeply than ever.

The carnival! The carnival! Is it any wonder that Tessa and her brother slept but little that night, and that when they did, they dreamed of processions and bonbons and clowns and flower-decked wagons and all sorts of strange sights?

Their father hired a donkey from one of his neighbours for Tessa and Francesca to ride on. Pietro was to carry their mother and the baby.

When at last they were ready to start, they were a merry sight. Beppo and Tessa had gathered quantities of wild flowers to use at the carnival, so that Tessa and her mother looked as though they were in the middle of travelling gardens.

"If these give out," Beppo had told his sister, "we can go over to the Coliseum and get wallflowers and some other pretty blossoms that grow in the crevices of the walls. They must be in bloom by this time. We must throw many a bouquet to Lucy and her brother."

The city looked bright and gay as the peasant and his family drew near. The streets were filled with carriages; the sidewalks were lined with people; while the houses were decked with bright-coloured carpets, mats, and all sorts of hangings.

Merry parties had already seated themselves in the balconies, for it was one o'clock on the first day of the carnival.

What does this word "carnival" mean? you ask. It is another name for "farewell to meat," and the great festival of Italy is always held during the week before the beginning of Lent. All the days except Sunday and Friday are given up to merrymaking, which grows more and more lively until the last night.

The children go to bed and get up whenever they like. There is no scolding, no cross word; and even if the sport becomes very rough, every one takes it with good nature.

Tessa and Beppo went with the rest of the family to their cousin's home on the ground floor of a tall stone building. But they rested only a few moments.

"Take the donkeys, children, and ride off to see the sights," said their father. "Your mother and I will stay and talk with our friends awhile before we go out."

They did not need to be told twice, and were soon in the midst of a merry crowd on the Corso, as one of the principal streets of Rome is called.

"Look, look, Beppo," said Tessa. "Do see that wagon full of clowns and queerly dressed people. They are having great sport. They are pelting every one with confetti. We shall get hit if we don't take care."

"We'll get some confetti ourselves," answered Beppo. "We must not wait any longer."

The two children stopped their donkeys in front of a stand covered with tiny lime-balls. Perhaps you would call them plaster candies. They were no larger than peas, and looked nice enough to eat.

crowd in street "WERE SOON IN THE MIDST OF A MERRY CROWD"
 "Now for fun," said Beppo, when each had purchased a big bag of confetti.

At this moment, some boys, who were close behind, gave Pietro's tail a sudden pull and Tessa fell forward as he jumped about. Before she could get up, she felt a shower of confetti falling over her neck and shoulders.

A loud laugh went up from the bystanders. Tessa laughed, too, as she brushed the powdery balls to right and left.

A moment after, another shower came falling about her. But this time it was made of sugar almonds, which a little girl was scattering from a balcony. She must have liked Tessa's pretty face and wished to give her a treat.

There was a great scrambling for the candy. The mischievous boys who had thrown the confetti got most of it, I fear, but Tessa enjoyed it, nevertheless.

"Look at the lovely carriage ahead of us," she cried. "It is lined with white. Aren't the ladies in it pretty, Beppo? That seat in front of them is just loaded with bouquets and confetti. They are standing up now to throw better."

Beppo didn't care for this half as much as for the wagon-loads of people dressed in bright colours and wearing masks.

"Look at that man, Tessa, before he is out of sight. Yes, it must be a man, though he is dressed like a woman. See his false curls hanging down under the bonnet, and hear him talk. He keeps every one around him laughing. Let's put on our masks and then ride past Lucy's house. She won't know us if she sees us."

Beppo had made some rude masks before the children left home. After they had put them on, they felt sure no one would know them as they rode through the lively crowd.

"Look up at the second balcony," whispered Tessa, as she came up close to her brother's side. "There are Lucy and Arthur with their father and mother, in the midst of a merry party. We might have known they would be here on the Corso."

"Do you see what Arthur is doing?" replied Beppo. "He has a bouquet of flowers fastened to the end of a long string. And now he is dangling it over the rail. Just see that lady in the balcony below reaching out to get it. She thinks it is being thrown to her. How surprised she is when it comes up again out of her reach. Oh, what sport!

"But watch, Tessa. I am going to throw my prettiest bunch of flowers to Lucy. Ah! she looks like an angel to-day. She is all in white."

Beppo took a bouquet of roses and tossed them straight up into his little friend's lap. She was looking directly toward him as he threw them. She began to laugh, and, lifting them in her hands, turned to her father and said something.

"She is asking him who we are," said Beppo. "She will never guess, for she does not expect to see us at the carnival."

Tessa and her brother now moved onward, but not before they were covered with a shower of candy. It was Lucy's return for her flowers.

A little before sunset the two country children went back to their cousin's. They found their father and mother all ready to go out to see the races.

"What an odd-looking child you are, Tessa. And you, too, Beppo," said their mother. For they were fairly covered with white dust.

"Never mind," laughed Beppo. "You will look like that to-morrow, mother, if you stay outdoors long enough. I really think that hundreds of bushels of confetti have been thrown about the streets to-day. We have received our share of them, without doubt."

"Come, come, not a moment to lose now," said the father, "or we shall be too late to see the sport."

The good-natured cousin said she would look after the baby, while Francesca rode off down the street on her father's shoulder. The donkeys had been put in the stable for their night's rest.

The party soon reached the Corso, which had been cleared of carriages. Both sides were lined by an ever-growing crowd.

Just at sunset a gun was fired. Instantly a number of beautiful horses were freed. They wore fine trappings and were without riders or drivers. Down the Corso they raced from one end to the other. It seemed as though they passed by like lightning.

"Good, good," shouted Beppo, as the first horse reached the goal. This one was the winner of the race, of course.

"We can see this sport every night of the carnival," his father told him, as they walked slowly homeward, looking at the sights on the way.

Early the next morning Tessa and Beppo started off on their donkeys once more. They did not wish to lose a moment of the day's fun. They had many a mock battle with the children whom they met, but the fighting was all good-natured, and the only weapons used were handfuls of confetti.

In the afternoon they found themselves near Arthur and Lucy, who were in an open carriage. They did not have their masks on, so their friends spied them out very quickly. They were very glad to see each other, but the crowd was so great they did not have a chance to say much.

"Tessa," whispered Lucy, "father has something to ask your parents. He was going to write to them if he did not see them before the end of the carnival. Be sure to tell them. It is about you."

That was all she had a chance to say before the driver started up the horses and she had passed on. Tessa wondered what it could be about, but her mind was soon busy with the gay sights, and she forgot all about it till she reached home.

The last night of the carnival was the gayest time of all. As soon as it was dark, Tessa went with her father and mother and Beppo out into the streets. Every one carried a torch and tried to keep it lighted. At the same time he must try to put out as many other torches as possible.

How the lights danced up and down the streets! What a puffing and blowing there was all the time. Tessa no sooner got her torch lighted than some one came up from behind and put it out. Then she would cry, "Senza moccolo, senza moccolo." That means, "Without light, without light."

After a while, Beppo fastened his torch to the end of a long pole. He thought he was safe at last. But, no! a moment afterward some one came along with a pole longer than his own and dashed it down. The fun was all the greater for such little things as this.

The city looked wonderfully pretty with the lights dancing about the windows and balconies and streets.

After an hour or two the crowds began to thin out. Every one was tired. Tessa and Beppo turned homeward with their father and mother, calling out:

"The carnival is dead. The carnival is dead."

Soon afterward they tumbled into bed, half asleep, still repeating the words they heard echoing through the streets:

"The carnival is dead!"

CHAPTER IX

THE BURIED CITY

"We should like to take your little daughter with us on a journey," said Mr. Gray to Tessa's father.

The two men were standing in the doorway of the artist's home on the Monday after the carnival. Tessa had not forgotten to tell her father that Mr. Gray wished to see him.

"We shall be gone only a few days. We are going to take a short trip to Naples," the artist went on. "But Lucy wishes Tessa's company very much, and I think your little girl would enjoy it. What do you say?"

The peasant was greatly pleased. His face beamed, as he replied:

"You are a good friend to us, Mr. Gray. We can never forget it. What shall we do when you go back to America?"

"That time will not come for two years yet. In the meanwhile, talk with your wife. If she is willing, bring Tessa here Tuesday morning. We shall leave on the afternoon of that day."

You can imagine how excited our little Italian cousin was, when she found herself riding on a train for the first time. The cars were much smaller than we use here in America. It would have seemed odd to you to have the conductor (or the guard, as he is called in Europe) lock the doors when the train is about to start.

"We are prisoners," laughed Lucy. "We can't get out now, even if we should wish to do so ever so much."

She was now able to chatter in Italian almost as fast as in her own English tongue.

"That is because of her acquaintance with Tessa and her brother," Mr. Gray told his wife. "Those children surprise me by the good Italian they speak, when they have had so little schooling. Although their parents are peasants, they are gentle people in their nature. And that is more than learning, after all."

The children were delighted with Naples. The city rests on the shore of what some people consider the most beautiful bay in the world. Everything about it looked clean and orderly, although a few years ago it was a very filthy city.

No one seemed in a hurry. Even the beggars, who came to meet the children with hands stretched out for alms, looked lazy and happy.

There were beautiful gardens to walk in, and fine buildings to visit, besides rowing and sailing on the blue waters of the bay. There was plenty to see, but best of all was the morning the children spent in the museum, where there was a large collection of curiosities.

"They all came from the buried city," Mr. Gray explained.

"Think of it, children! These beautiful ornaments, vases, and bronzes, were hidden under the ashes for eighteen hundred years. One day it was discovered by some workman that he was digging into the ruins of a building. Others came to help him, and by and by they found a city beneath the ashes and soil which had formed above it."

"You are going to take us to see the city before we go back to Rome, aren't you, father?" asked Arthur.

"Certainly; I would not have you miss the sight for a good deal. But does Tessa know its name?"

"O yes, it is Pompeii. I have heard much about it," the little Italian answered. "It is another of the wonderful sights in my country of which I am so proud."

The children passed slowly from one part of the museum to another. They examined the almonds, dates, and figs, which had been preserved so long. Some of them looked quite natural. There was a lady's toilet set that interested the girls very much.

There were blackened loaves of bread and cake from the baker's oven; there were beautiful lamps and golden jewelry,—all these things made for people suddenly overtaken by death nearly two thousand years ago!

It was hard to leave the museum.

"But there are other things to see yet, and we cannot spend too much time in one place," Mr. Gray told them as they walked homeward.

They stopped to buy some luscious yellow oranges and some ornaments of coral and lava at stands by the side of the street.

That very evening ponies were brought to the hotel door, and the party started out to climb the side of Vesuvius.

"I shouldn't think the people of Naples would feel safe to live so near a volcano," said Lucy. "Now that it is active again, it must make them think of the way Pompeii was destroyed. And Pompeii is several miles away, isn't it, father?"

"Yes, there was no more thought of danger at that time than we feel to-night. Perhaps not so much," he added, as he looked toward his wife.

She was a little pale and was feeling more timid than she liked to say. Up above them, even now, they could see the sky lighted up by the red flame. It looked as though a city must be on fire. The path wound in a roundabout way, but was always rising and was in some places very steep and rocky.

"See that red stream of lava pouring down the side of the mountain," said Arthur.

It was not so far away but that the children could see men at work beside it. They were scooping the lava up into vessels. It would be taken down to Naples and made into jewelry and ornaments to be sold to visitors in the city.

After two miles or more of hard climbing, they reached the side of the crater.

"Don't go too near. Oh, do be careful, children," cried Mrs. Gray. She was trembling as she looked at the red-hot stones flying upward in the midst of the cinders and flames.

"Listen, do listen, mother. It is grand!" said Lucy, as they could now hear the roaring and grumbling, the pounding and hammering under ground. It was as though some terrible being was an angry prisoner in the volcano and was trying to free himself.

Tessa clung to Mrs. Gray's skirt at first. She was frightened, too, and it was no wonder. But after a few moments both she and her kind friend had got over their fright and had begun to enjoy the strange sight.

ruins "IT WAS A STRANGE PLACE"
When at last Mrs. Gray said it was time to go, they all felt sorry.

The drive down the mountain was quite easy. When they reached the hotel the children went straight to bed to dream of the pleasure to-morrow,—for they were to visit the buried city, Pompeii.

The next day was bright and clear. Although every one felt a little tired after the excitement of the night before, they were all ready for the day's trip.

It was a strange place, this city with no one living in it. There were streets all laid out and the walls of houses standing. The roofs were gone, however.

Mr. Gray explained to the children that the city was buried under the terrible shower of ashes which settled down over it. The roofs had been burnt or broken down by the weight above them. After a while, soil formed above the ashes, grass began to grow, and the rest of the world forgot about the city, once so beautiful, with its stately palaces and grand buildings.

Most of the people had time to flee before their homes were destroyed. But some of them stayed too long. Their skeletons were found when the city was unearthed.

The children went into a cellar where there were marks on the walls. The guide told them that these showed where people were pressed against them. They must have fled to that place for safety, but it had been of no use. They stood here prisoners until kind death freed them from their suffering.

They saw many marble ornaments. There were ducks and geese, rabbits and lambs, made long ago.

"All this makes me feel queer, Lucy," whispered Tessa. "I will be glad to get back to a live city again." Lucy felt so, too. It was interesting, of course, but it was very strange.

After the visit to Pompeii, Mr. Gray told the children that his vacation was over and they must all go back to Rome.

"But we will not return by train," he said. "We will take a sailing vessel, as I think you will enjoy a trip on the water."

They did enjoy it greatly. The only trouble was that it seemed too short.

"When June comes it will be quite hot in Rome, you know," Lucy said to Tessa. The two girls were in the bow of the boat, looking over the edge into the water below.

"We are going then on a journey to the north of Italy, and you are to come, too, Tessa. Father says so. We will visit Venice and sail in boats through its streets. It seems as though I could hardly wait for the time to come. Just think of a great city built on little islands, and when you go to the door of your house you find yourself on the water's edge. It must be lovely."

"Tessa," she went on, putting her arm around the little Italian's waist, "father says that he is going to manage next winter so that you shall stay with us and we can have lessons together with my governess."

Tessa bent forward and kissed both of Lucy's hands. She was so happy she could not speak.

THE END